Merrill

Oceanus
Dragonicus

mountains

Dragon Island

Murdoch's Adventure Atlas of the Known and Unknown World

Caves

volcanoes

For Jessica,

there are some things you just know

—J. N.

For Tom and Karen

—E. P.

ISBN 0-439-07726-5

Text copyright © 1998 by Jerdine Nolen.
Illustrations copyright © 1998 by Elise Primavera.
All rights reserved. Published by Scholastic Inc., 555 Broadway,
New York, NY 10012, by arrangement with Harcourt Brace & Company.
SCHOLASTIC and associated logos are trademarks and/or registered
trademarks of Scholastic Inc.

12 11 10 9 8 7 6 5 4 3 2 1   9/9 0 1 2 3 4/0

Printed in the U.S.A.   14

First Scholastic printing, March 1999

The illustrations in this book were done in acrylic paints
and pastels on gessoed illustration board.
The display type was set in Latin Wide.
The text type was set in Perpetua.
Designed by Camilla Filancia

Raising Dragons

Jerdine Nolen
Raising

Dragons

ILLUSTRATED BY **Elise Primavera**

SCHOLASTIC INC.
New York   Toronto   London   Auckland   Sydney
Mexico City   New Delhi   Hong Kong

PA DIDN'T KNOW a thing about raising
dragons. He raised corn and peas and barley and wheat.
He raised sheep and cows and pigs and chickens. He raised
just about everything we needed for life on our farm, but he
didn't know a thing about raising dragons.

Ma didn't know about dragons, either. She made a real nice home for us. But
when it came to dragons, she didn't even know what they wanted for dessert!

Now me, I knew everything about dragons, and I knew they were real.

At first Pa thought the notion of dragons on a farm was just plain foolishness.
"I'm not too particular about fanciful critters. And, I don't have any time for
make-believe," he told me one day. So when Pa said he didn't want to talk
anymore, I knew I'd better keep my opinions to myself. I did my chores
with my thoughts in my head at one end of the barn while
Pa worked at the other end with his thoughts.

I remember the day my life with dragons began.
I was out for my Sunday-before-supper walk. Near
Miller's cave I came across something that looked like a big
rock. But it was too round and too smooth—not hard enough to
be a rock.
Carefully I rolled it into the cave and went to fetch Pa.
"What do you think it is, Pa?"
"An egg. A big egg" was all he said. "Now you stay away from
that thing, daughter. No telling what'll come out of it!"
I couldn't tell if Pa was more scared than worried.
"You just stay away, you hear me!"
he said, pointing a finger.

I always minded my parents, never had a reason not to. And I tried to mind Pa now, but I could not stay away. Day after day I'd go to Miller's cave to wait and watch, and wonder: *What is coming out of that egg?*

One night I couldn't sleep. I got out of my bed and climbed out of my window onto the perch Pa had made for me in the oak tree.

But a loud noise broke the stillness of the night. *Crack!* It was louder than one hundred firecrackers on the Fourth of July. *CRACK!* I heard it again, this time louder than before. It was coming from Miller's cave. At the first hint of dawn, I headed toward that sound.

There in the corner of the cave, where I'd left it, was the egg. And pushing its way out, like I've seen so many baby chicks do, was a tiny dragon poking through that shell with its snout.

It was love at first sight.

"Hey there, li'l feller, welcome to the world," I sang, soft and low. As I stroked his nose, a sweet little purring whimper came from him. As I touched skin to scale, I knew I was his girl and he was my dragon. I named him Hank.

Hank was just a joy to have around. He was a fire-breathing dragon, and he made sure he kept his temper whenever I was near.

Pa wouldn't have seen the sense or the use of having a dragon around who ate you out of house and home. Thankfully, Hank preferred fish, frogs, eels, and insects to beef, lamb, chicken, and pork. And he *did* have a healthy appetite!

Ma never wanted to know about Hank. Whenever I wanted to talk about him, she'd cover her ears and sing. She said that having a dragon around had to be worse than having a field full of critters. But it wasn't.

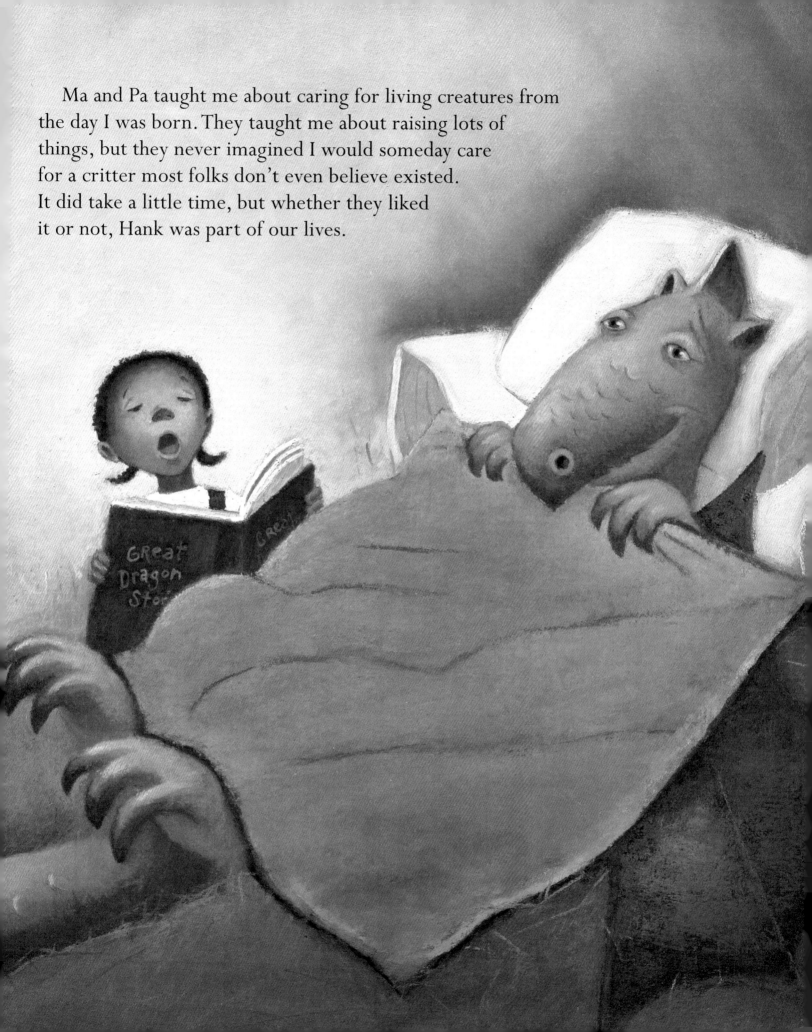

Ma and Pa taught me about caring for living creatures from the day I was born. They taught me about raising lots of things, but they never imagined I would someday care for a critter most folks don't even believe existed. It did take a little time, but whether they liked it or not, Hank was part of our lives.

He was an awesome thing. Growing
to be as big as the barn from tail to snout. Hank
was very clumsy when his wings came in. But once he
learned how to use them, we'd go flying, mostly at night.

Up until then I had been afraid of the dark. The shadows and
muffled noises and the complete quiet stillness always seemed to
be waiting and watching me. I had seen our farm from up in my
tree perch. But Hank showed me my world from on high, the way
a cloud or a bird or a star just might be seeing me. Up there
I saw things for what they were. And it was just grand!

Pa was the first one to notice what he called a strangeness happening around our farm. One morning with Samson, our mule, hitched for work, Pa set out to plow the fields. But all the work had been done. The ground was turned over and seeds had been sown. Pa was plumb flabbergasted!

Hank and I tended the crops, too. We pulled weeds and kept varmints away. And Hank even got me to school before the first bell.

Even after all the good he'd done, Ma still didn't want any part of Hank. But when a hot spell hit, her tomatoes began to dry out. Hank hovered above them, fanning away the heat. He saved just about every last one of them. Ma didn't admit it, but she felt beholden to Hank. She began fixing fancy gourmet meals just for him—eel potpies, frog-leg pudding, and a fish-and-insect stew that Hank just loved.

Day by day Hank was getting bigger. Ma was uneasy about Hank's fire-breathing breath.

Pa paced with worry about all the corn Hank and I planted. There was corn growing *everywhere*. Ma cooked as much of it as she could, but there was too much. Just when it seemed like the corn would swallow up our farm, Hank grabbed Pa's shovel and dug a wide trench around the cornfield. Then he blew on it with his hot breath.

"What in tarnation?" Pa screamed. Ma ran out of the house carrying a bucket of water. But it was too late. The whole field was ablaze. We couldn't believe our ears—POP! POP!! Pop, Pop! POP!—or our eyes.

Hank was making popcorn. It took an entire week to salt and bag it. We sold it all—at a profit. It was the first dragon-popped popcorn anybody ever saw or tasted. Oh, it was *real* good, too.

When Ma harvested her tomatoes,
Nancy Akins bought some. She claimed they
had medicinal value. She said they cured her gout.
Pretty soon folks wanted dragon-grown food like they
wanted medicine or magic cures. But there was nothing
medicinal or magical about it. It was just Hank.

The crowds and attention decided his fate. One evening
Ma and I were sitting in front of our potbellied stove. She was
shelling peas while I read *Murdoch's Adventure Atlas of the Known
and Unknown World*, a book I'd got from the library that morning. In
that instant I realized what I needed to do.

Come morning, Hank and I set out for the dragon-shaped
landmass floating in the middle of the ocean.

There were dragons everywhere.
They put us up in their best hotel, invited
us to eat in their best restaurants. Hank felt right at home.
When I saw Hank playing run-and-fly-and-chase, I knew he
had found the perfect place to be.
All in all, it was a great vacation.

But at the end, it got real hard: I had to say
farewell to Hank. At least for now.

Normally I don't get mushy at departing, but when
Hank turned to me and called me Cupcake, I *boohoo*ed a heap.

Just as I was about to board my plane, Hank stood there on the
runway trying to hide a wheelbarrow behind his back. His toothy grin
lit up that cloudy day. That wheelbarrow was full of . . .

"ROCKS??" Ma squealed in puzzlement.
"'Tain't rocks, Mother. They're eggs,
dragon eggs!" I exclaimed.
Pa beamed right proud.
Each egg looked different from the rest:
One glowed, one glistened, another one flickered,
and one even sparkled. I stood admiring the lot of them.
Looking at those eggs, I thought about my Hank. For now,
he was out there somewhere in the world. I knew I'd see him
again. Wondering *when* was the only thing fixed in my mind.
But in the meantime, I knew what I had to do. The same
way Pa knew that farming was in his blood, I knew
that raising dragons was in mine.

There are some things you just know.

Oceanus Dragonicus

mountains

Dragon Island

Murdoch's
Adventure Atlas
of the
Known
and
Unknown
World

Caves

volcanoes